White Tiger, Blue Serpent

For my mother and father
—G. T.

For Grace and Michael
May you live happily ever after together.
—J. & M. T.

Watercolors and natural pigments were used for the full-color illustrations.
The text type is 14-point Classical Garamond.

Text copyright © 1999 by Grace Tseng
Illustrations copyright © 1999 by Jean and Mou-sien Tseng

Published by Lothrop, Lee & Shepard Books
a division of William Morrow and Company, Inc.
1350 Avenue of the Americas, New York, NY 10019
www.williammorrow.com

Printed in Hong Kong by South China Printing Company (1988) Ltd.

10 9 8 7 6 5 4 3 2 1

Library of Congress Cataloging-in-Publication Data
Tseng, Grace.
White tiger, blue serpent / by Grace Tseng; illustrated by Jean and Mou-sien Tseng.
p. cm.
Summary: When his mother's beautiful brocade is snatched
away by a greedy goddess, a young Chinese boy faces
many perils as he attempts to get it back.
ISBN 0-688-12515-8 (trade)—ISBN 0-688-12516-6 (library)
[1. Fairy tales.   2. China—Fiction.]   I. Tseng, Jean, ill.
II. Tseng, Mou-sien, ill.   III. Title.   PZ8.T7938Br
1999   [E]—DC20   94-9757   CIP AC

White Tiger, Blue Serpent is based
on a tale from the Drung tribe
of the Yunnan Province
in southwest China.

White Tiger, Blue Serpent

GRACE TSENG

ILLUSTRATED BY

JEAN AND MOU-SIEN TSENG

Lothrop, Lee & Shepard Books

NEW YORK

A long time ago, in a remote region of China, a great river ran its course between two very different lands. On its east bank was a land of magical mountains. Its thick forests dripped with exotic fruit. Playful monkeys, regal pheasants, and exotic lizards made their homes in its valleys. Swirling clouds crowned its mountain peaks.

Despite its beauty, no one from the west dared to enter this land, for it was said that the goddess Qin, feared for her jealous temper, lived there, guarded by a ferocious white tiger and a monstrous blue serpent. So although a bridge stretched across the roaring river that divided the two lands, no one ever set foot on it.

The west bank of the river was like another world. There the land was rocky and infertile, the forests dark and empty.

On this unlucky side of the river, a tiny cottage stood alone on the shore. Inside lived a young boy named Kai and his mother. They were very poor, and their lives were filled with hard work.

Kai's job was to fish. Every day he rose before the sun to throw his line into the great river. But the raging waters carried the fish by so quickly, they rarely had time to notice Kai's line, and it often took him until after dark to catch dinner.

While Kai was fishing, his mother sat at her loom weaving magnificent silk brocades. As her skilled fingers flew, glorious chrysanthemums, elegant birds, and curious fish came to life in the delicate threads. Each brocade took many months to complete, and with each passing week it became harder for Kai to part with. Yet, although it broke his heart to lose them, the brocades had to be traded for rice and firewood and weaving silk.

"Please, Mother," Kai begged one night as his mother completed another brocade, "couldn't we keep this one for us to enjoy? I will catch more fish so that we have some left over to trade for silk. I will gather firewood from the forest. Perhaps I could even plant rice. Anything so we do not have to trade away another brocade."

His mother was silent. For many years she had yearned to make a special brocade for her dear son, but to do so would mean much hard work for Kai—work for a grown man, not for a young boy. The look in his eyes finally persuaded her.

"I *will* make you a brocade," she told him at last. "It will take me a thousand days and a thousand nights, but when it is done, it will be the most beautiful brocade I have ever made."

The following day Kai took the newest brocade to market. He bought only half the rice he usually did, and he bought no firewood at all. With the money left over, he purchased an ax and some rice seedlings.

The next morning Kai and his mother rose much earlier than usual. Still, by the time Kai caught a fish, it was already midday. He ran with it back to the cottage.

Then, without resting, he picked up the ax and rushed to the forest to chop firewood. The ax was heavy for a small boy like Kai, and by the time he finished chopping the night's firewood, the sun had already set.

And so it was by lantern light that Kai plowed and flooded a small rice field and planted the seedlings he had bought.

Slowly the days passed, and as they did, Kai began to change. Where at first the racing fish were but a blur before Kai's eyes, as time went on he became faster than they were. Eventually he no longer needed his fishing pole at all. When a fish swam close to shore, he just reached into the water and grabbed it.

Chopping firewood became less tedious, too. The ax grew lighter and lighter, until one day Kai no longer needed it either. He had grown so strong, he could pull a tree right out of the ground with his bare hands.

And the rice field? At first Kai worked by lantern light. But gradually his sight became so sharp, he could see the tiny rice grains on even the blackest night.

Finally the thousandth day arrived and the brocade was finished. The townspeople, who had all heard of its magnificence, rushed to the tiny cottage. As there were too many people to fit inside, Kai's mother had to bring the brocade outdoors. A hush fell over the crowd when they saw it. Woven in the finest silk were a brilliant sun and a glowing moon, mighty mountains and bubbling rivers, trees lush with fruit, a vibrant rainbow, flowers in every color imaginable, glistening fish, jumping grasshoppers, animals of all shapes and sizes skipping and running and flying. Never was there anything so beautiful!

Before the people had time to give voice to their praise, a gust of wind came out of nowhere. It circled the cottage and tore through the crowd. Then it found the brocade. Catching hold of it, the wind lifted the splendid creation into the air, higher and higher, across the river and into the magical mountains.

"It is the goddess Qin!" cried the people in terror, and a wail arose, for all were certain that the brocade was gone forever.

Kai watched with dismay. A thousand of his mother's days and a thousand of her nights were in that brocade. He would not stand here and see it stolen! As the townspeople watched in disbelief, he tore across the bridge, over the roaring river and into the fearful land.

Up the mountain paths he flew. The brocade was soon obscured by clouds, but Kai, whose sight was sharpened by tending rice at night, could see it clearly. Even after nightfall he pursued the brocade.

The next morning the brocade dropped into a dense forest on a mountain peak. Kai shuddered, for this, he knew, was the fabled home of the fierce white tiger. Yet he could not stop now. Higher up the mountain he ran, deeper and deeper into the forest, until he reached the glorious brocade. When he did, his steps froze. Sitting on it, more enormous and ferocious than Kai had ever imagined, was the white tiger.

Seeing Kai, the tiger stood and opened its giant mouth. The roar that came out shook the birds from the trees and made Kai tingle from head to toe. But gathering firewood had made him strong. As the tiger leaped, Kai yanked a big tree out of the ground, swung the trunk with all his strength, and knocked the tiger senseless.

Kai raced to grab the brocade. Just as his fingers touched the silken threads, the wind arose again and snatched it up.

Over the treetops the brocade flew, with Kai chasing after it on the ground.

Once again he ran all through the night. When morning broke, he found himself at the edge of a vast lake. The brocade was flying toward an island in the middle.

On the shore lay an old rowboat. Kai thrust it into the water and set off. But as fast as he could row, the water seemed to roll him back. It felt for all the world as if he were rowing up a mountain. Kai looked into the water. If this was a mountain, it was a mountain of blue scales! It was the serpent.

The serpent's monstrous head reared above the water. Its razor teeth flashed, its forked tongue cracked like a whip, its twisted horn aimed at Kai. With the speed Kai had learned from catching fish, he grabbed the horn and held on tight. The serpent thrashed its head and howled. Kai waited for the ideal moment and then let go. He sailed through the air and landed safely on the island's shore.

Quickly Kai scrambled to his feet and started up the mountain in the center of the island. At its top were two towering doors. Kai was about to pound on them when suddenly, silently, they opened. Standing before him was a beautiful maiden. Graciously she motioned for Kai to enter, then slammed the doors behind him with hardly a touch.

The maiden led Kai through countless rooms, each more splendid than the last. The floors were made of the greenest jade; the ceilings sparkled with jewels. At last they reached the grandest room of all.

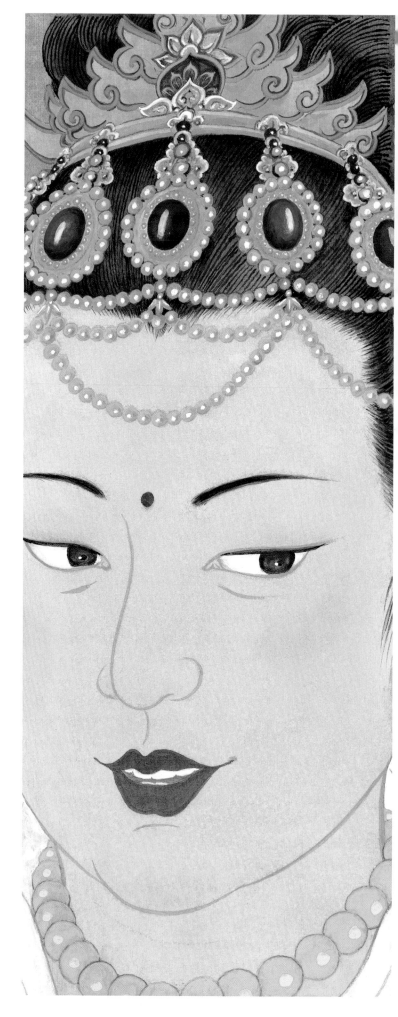

At its center a ring of beautiful maidens encircled the loveliest woman Kai had ever seen, and in her lap lay the brocade.

The goddess Qin looked up at Kai. "You have made your journey for nothing," she told him with a greedy smile. "Never have I seen so glorious a brocade, and I intend to keep it for myself."

Kai started toward her, but suddenly a mighty whirlwind sprang up before him— a whirlwind of the goddess's making. Although Kai fought with every bit of his strength, he could not move.

The wind grew stronger, pushing Kai backward, flinging furniture about the room, ripping tapestries from the walls. And then, just as Kai was sure his life was at an end, an amazing thing happened.

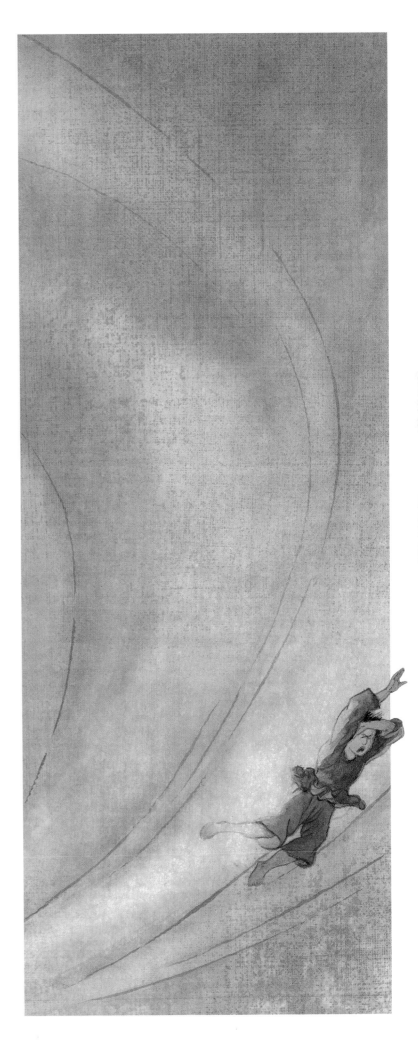

The whirlwind blew so hard that the creatures of the brocade were blown right off of it. Birds took flight, deer leaped forth, bears lumbered, peacocks screamed. Trees and flowers flew through the air. And beneath them all, a shining rainbow stretched itself out and formed a path for Kai and the rest. Over the palace walls the path led, across the dark lake, over the mountains, and back to the tiny cottage on the other side of the river. All that remained in the goddess's lap was a faded cloth full of holes.

Kai's mother ran from the cottage to greet her son and laughed in amazement at what she saw next. The fish took two jumps and landed in the river. The animals and birds and insects scampered away to find new homes. Flowers popped up everywhere. Trees planted themselves in the ground. And the sun smiled gently over the whole scene.

From that day forward, the two banks
of the great river stood balanced in their
brilliance and splendor, and Kai and
his mother lived peacefully and
happily in the beauty of the
magnificent brocade.